for
Félix

Copyright © 2004 by Bayard Éditions Jeunesse
Published by Roaring Brook Press
Roaring Brook Press is a division of Holtzbrinck Publishing Holdings Limited Partnership
175 Fifth Avenue, New York, New York 10010
All rights reserved
www.roaringbrookpress.com

Distributed in Canada by H. B. Fenn and Company, Ltd.

Cataloging-in-Publication Data is on file at the Library of Congress.
ISBN-13: 978-1-59643-496-7
ISBN-10: 1-59643-496-1

Roaring Brook Press books are available for special promotions and premiums.
For details contact:
Director of Special Markets, Holtzbrinck Publishers.

Printed in China
First American Edition May 2009
2 4 6 8 10 9 7 5 3 1

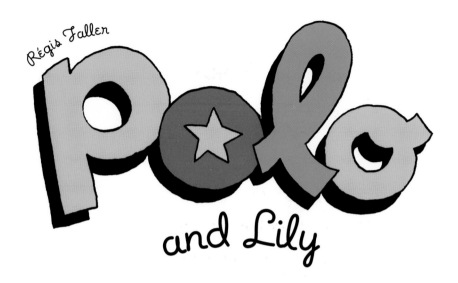

Régis Faller

Polo
and Lily

ROARING BROOK PRESS

NEW YORK

GLUG

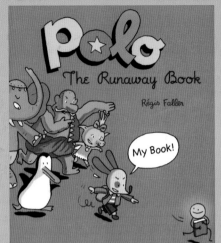

Discover Polo's world at: www.PolosHouse.com

And come back to Polo's house:

Polo and the Magic Flute
Polo and the Magician!
Polo and the Dragon
The Adventures of Polo
Polo: The Runaway Book